THE THREE BEARS
AND OTHER STORIES

RETOLD BY SUSAN PRICE

ILLUSTRATED BY MOIRA & COLIN MACLEAN

Kingfisher Books

Kingfisher Books, Grisewood & Dempsey Ltd,
Elsley House, 24–30 Great Titchfield Street, London W1P 7AD

First published in 1992 by Kingfisher Books.
4 6 8 10 9 7 5 3

The material in this edition was previously published by Kingfisher Books in
The Kingfisher Treasury of Nursery Stories (1990).

Text © Susan Price 1990, 1992
Illustrations © Colin and Moira Maclean 1990, 1992

BRITISH LIBRARY CATALOGUING IN PUBLICATION DATA
A catalogue record for this book is available from the British Library

ISBN 0 86272 892 4

Printed and bound in Spain

CONTENTS

◆ THE THREE BEARS ◆

Once upon a time, deep in a dark wood, lived three bears.

The biggest was Daddy Bear. The middling one was Mummy Bear. And the littlest one was Baby Bear.

Every morning they had porridge for breakfast. But one morning the porridge was too hot and burned their mouths. "Let's go for a walk in the wood," said Mummy Bear, "until the porridge is cool enough to eat."

"Good idea," said Daddy Bear. So they took Baby Bear's paws in theirs, and walked out in the wood.

Their little house was left empty, with three bowls of porridge cooling on the table.

Then, through the wood, came a little girl. She was lost and hungry, and her name was Goldilocks.

When she saw the little house she thought, "Oh, I wonder who lives there. Perhaps they can tell me how to find my way out of the wood. Perhaps they can give me something to eat." So she went up to the door of the little house and knocked.

But no one came to the door, even when she knocked again. She tried to look in at the window, but she wasn't tall enough. She called, but still no one came.

So she stood on tiptoe, and stretched up high, and opened the door, even though it wasn't her house! She went quietly inside and looked around.

No one was at home. But on the table stood those three bowls of porridge: a great big bowl, a middling-sized bowl and a tiny little bowl.

"I'm so hungry," thought Goldilocks, and there's no one here to ask. I'll just try this porridge."

First she went to the great big bowl. She dug in the spoon and took a big mouthful.

But it was HOT!

"Too hot! Too hot!" said Goldilocks, and she dropped the spoon back in the bowl.

She went to the middling-sized bowl and tried a spoonful of that. But it was sticky and COLD. Goldilocks made a face. "Too cold! Too cold!" she said.

And she dropped the spoon back in the bowl.

Then she tried the porridge in the littlest bowl. It was not too hot and not too cold, but just right! So she ate it all up and licked the bowl clean.

Goldilocks was tired because she'd walked so far. She saw three chairs against the wall: a great big chair, a middling-sized chair and a tiny little chair.

First she climbed onto the great big chair, but it was too hard, and she slid off again.

Then Goldilocks tried the middling-sized chair, but that was too soft, and she soon scrambled off.

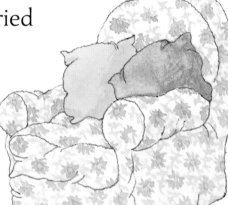

But when she sat in the tiny little chair, it wasn't too hard and it wasn't too soft. It was just right, so she thought, "I'll sit here for a while."

But just as Goldilocks thought that, the tiny little chair broke, and she fell on the floor!

When she got up she was cross, and still tired. So she went upstairs, even though it wasn't her house, and found a room with three beds.

There was a great big bed, a

middling-sized bed and a tiny little bed. Goldilocks tried the great big bed first, but it was too hard. So she rolled off it and tried the middling-sized bed, but it was too soft.

So she left that one and tried the tiny little bed. Now that bed wasn't too hard and it wasn't too soft. It was just right! Goldilocks fell fast asleep.

While she was asleep, the three bears came home from their walk in the wood. They looked at their porridge bowls, and Daddy Bear saw that a big spoonful had been taken from his bowl.

In his great big bear's voice, he growled, "Who's been eating my porridge?"

In her soft, middling voice, Mummy Bear said, "And who's been eating my porridge?"

In her tiny little voice, Baby Bear said, "Who's been eating my porridge, and has eaten it all up?"

Then Daddy Bear saw that his chair had been moved and he roared, "Who's been sitting on my chair?"

And Mummy Bear said, "Who's been sitting on my chair?"

Baby Bear began to cry, "Who's been sitting in my chair, and has broken it all up?"

Then the three bears went upstairs. In his great big voice, Daddy Bear said, "Who's been sleeping in my bed?" And Mummy Bear said, "Who's been sleeping in my bed?" Then Baby Bear cried, "Who's been sleeping in my bed and is still in it?"

Mummy Bear and Daddy Bear came to look. There lay Goldilocks, snoring in the little bed. But the sound of Baby Bear crying woke her, and she sat up.

When she saw three bears looking at her, she was so frightened that she jumped right out of the window. Luckily she landed in soft grass, so she wasn't hurt. She ran and ran and ran. Soon she was out of the wood, and then she knew her way home. Goldilocks never came back, and lived happily ever after.

As for the three bears, whenever they went for a walk after that, they remembered to lock their door, so no one could creep in, eat their porridge or break their chairs. So they lived happily ever after too. Everyone was happy. And that's the end.

THE
◆ ENORMOUS TURNIP ◆

Once upon a time there was an old man who planted a turnip seed in the ground and waited for it to grow.

First it grew into a small turnip, then into a middling turnip, then a big turnip, then a bigger turnip and then an enormous turnip! The old man decided that it was time to pull the turnip up and eat it.

So he took hold of the turnip and pulled. But the turnip stayed in the ground.

The old man took a better grip and pulled harder. The turnip still stayed in the ground.

Then the old man gritted his teeth and pulled and pulled and pulled, until he had no pull left in him. But the turnip stayed in the ground.

So the old man went to his wife and said, "Wife, come and help me pull up this turnip."

So the old woman went with him back to the turnip. She took hold of the old man, the old man took hold of the turnip and they pulled. They pulled again.

They pulled and they pulled and they pulled, until they had no pull left in them. And the turnip stayed in the ground.

So the old woman went and found her granddaughter and said, "Granddaughter, come and help us pull up this turnip."

The granddaughter went back with the old woman. She took hold of the old woman, the old woman took hold of the old man, the old man took hold of the turnip and they got ready.

"Now let's try tugging," said the old man.

So they tugged.

They TUGGED and they TUGGED and they TUGGED, until none of them had any tug left. And the turnip stayed in the ground.

So the granddaughter went and found the dog. "Dog," she said, "come and help us tug this turnip up."

The dog went with the girl back to the turnip.

The dog took hold of the girl, the girl took hold of the old woman, the old woman took hold of the old man, the old man took hold of the turnip, and they all got ready.

"Let's try heaving," said the old man.

So they heaved at the turnip.

They HEAVED,
and they HEAVED,
and they HEAVED.

HEAVE . . .

HEAVE . . .

HEAVE . . . until none of them had any heave left in them. And the turnip stayed in the ground.

So the dog went away and found the cat and said, "Cat, come and help us heave at this turnip."

The cat went with the dog, and took hold of the dog. The dog took hold of the girl, the girl took hold of the old woman, the old woman took hold of the old man, the old man took hold of the turnip, and they all got ready. "Let's try dragging it this time."

So they dragged at the turnip.

They dragged again.

And the turnip came up out of the ground!

And the cat fell on the ground, the dog fell on the cat, the girl fell on the dog, the old woman fell on her granddaughter and the old man fell on his wife, and the turnip fell on the old man.

It took all of them to pull, tug, heave and drag the turnip to the house. There they cut it up and made it into turnip soup. There was more than enough for everyone, and for all I know, the old man, the old woman, their grand-daughter, the dog and the cat have lived on turnip soup from that day to this, and are all eating huge bowlfuls of turnip soup this very minute, even as you are listening to this story.

But that's enough of turnips, and the end of the story.

THE ELVES AND THE SHOEMAKER

Once upon a time there was a poor shoemaker. He was a good shoemaker, but there were many other shoemakers in the town, and no matter how hard he worked, he couldn't sell enough shoes to feed his family. Soon he had only one small bit of leather left, and no money to buy any more.

"Without leather, I can't make shoes," he said to his wife. "And if I can't make shoes, I can't sell any. And if I don't sell any shoes, we shan't have any money to buy food. We shall go hungry, you and our children and I."

"Well," said his wife, "make one last pair of shoes with that last bit of leather."

The shoemaker did as his wife said, and cut out the pieces. He didn't have time to sew the shoes together that night, so he left the pieces lying on his workbench.

The next morning, when he came back to his workbench to finish the shoes, he found they'd already been finished! There on the workbench was a beautiful

pair of shoes! He picked them up and looked at them. The stitches were so tiny they couldn't be seen. The seams were so smooth they would never rub. They were the very best pair of shoes the shoemaker had ever seen.

"But how did they get here?" he asked himself. "Who made them?"

Since the shoes *were* there, and since they were so fine, the shoemaker put them in his shop window. A rich gentleman came in and bought them right away – for more money than the shoemaker had ever been paid before.

The shoemaker's wife was able to buy food for the family, and the shoemaker bought more leather to make more shoes. All day long he worked, cutting out pairs of shoes. That night he left all the pieces on his workbench, ready to sew in the morning, and went to bed, tired out.

The next morning, the shoemaker came back to his workbench and found that all his work had been done for him, again! All the pieces he had left on his bench the night before had been sewn together, much more cleverly than the shoemaker himself could have done it. The shoemaker put the shoes in his window, and by that night he had sold them all, for good prices.

And so it went on. The shoemaker cut out shoes during the day; and during the night someone came and sewed them together. The shoemaker didn't know who was doing the work, but whoever it was, there wasn't a better shoemaker in town.

Soon everyone was coming to the shop to buy their shoes. The shoemaker was famous. And he was rich.

Just before Christmas, the shoemaker had an idea.

"Wife," he said, "don't you think it would be a good idea to stay up one night, and find out who is helping us?"

His wife agreed. So that night, instead of going to bed, they hid in the workroom and waited.

At midnight there was a sound of tiny feet, like the sound that mice make. But it wasn't mice that ran across the floor – it was two tiny men. They climbed up onto the

workbench and set to work, with needles as big as themselves and reels of thread that were a lot bigger.

"Elves!" the shoemaker whispered. "Elves have been helping us."

"Poor little things," said his wife. "They haven't a stitch on. They must be cold. Husband, let's make them clothes!"

So the next day the shoemaker's wife went out and bought little pieces of the best velvets and silks she could find. All week long she cut and sewed, doing her best to make the finest little suits with the neatest little stitches. Little velvet jackets and breeches, tiny silk shirts and stockings she made, while the shoemaker used the softest leather to make tiny little shoes.

On Christmas Eve they finished the gifts, wrapped them up and left them on the workbench. Then they hid, to see what the elves would say when they found the presents. At midnight, the elves ran across the floor and up onto the workbench. When they unwrapped the clothes, they put them on at once, and danced about admiring each other.

"Why, brother," said one elf, "we can't work at a greasy old shoemaker's bench in velvet and silk!"

"I shall never work again!" said the other. "Not now I'm so fine!" The two little elves jumped down from the workbench and ran away. They never came back.

But by now the shoemaker was so famous for his wonderful shoes that he still did good business. No one noticed that his stitches were not quite so tiny nor his seams so smooth, and he and his family were never poor again.